Enid Blyton

Run-About's
Holiday

Text illustrations by Brian Lee
Cover illustration by Alan Fredman

D1098248

AWARD PUBLICATIONS LIMITED

Enid Blyton's Happy Days!

Snowball the Pony

Bimbo and Topsy

Run-About's Holiday

The Adventures of Binkle and Flip

Binkle and Flip Misbehave

Mister Meddle's Mischief

Mister Meddle's Muddles

Merry Mister Meddle

You're a Nuisance Mister Meddle

Collect all the titles in the series!

The Adventures of
Mr Pink-Whistle

**Mr Pink-Whistle
Has Some Fun**

**Mr Pink-Whistle's
Party**

**Mr Pink-Whistle
Interferes**

Hello
Mr Twiddle!

**Mr Twiddle
in Trouble Again**

Don't Be Silly,
Mr Twiddle!

**Mr Twiddle
in Trouble Again**

**Shuffle
the Shoemaker**

For further information on Enid Blyton please visit *www.blyton.com*

ISBN 978-1-84135-657-0

First published 1955 by Lutterworth Press

First published by Award Publications Limited 2004
This edition first published 2010

Published by Award Publications Limited,
The Old Riding School, The Welbeck Estate,
Worksop, Nottinghamshire, S80 3LR

11 2

Printed in the United Kingdom

Contents

good

Chapter 1

The Funny Little Man

It all began on the day when Robin and Betty left their little wooden engine and its trucks out on the lawn.

They had hurried in to their dinner – and had forgotten all about the red engine and its coloured wooden trucks. They didn't go out to play afterwards because it began to rain.

Suddenly Robin remembered the little train and went to the window. 'Betty – we left the wooden train out on the grass!' he said. 'It will get wet and the paint will be spoilt, I'll go and bring it in.'

'I'll come with you,' said Betty. 'Let's put on our macs and sou'westers – it's nice to go out in the rain!'

great

7

So out they went, down the garden to the lawn where they had been playing. 'We left the train here,' said Robin, looking all round. 'Where's it gone?'

It wasn't there. 'We *did* leave it here, didn't we?' said Robin, puzzled. Then he suddenly caught sight of a bit of bright red under a bush. 'Oh, there it is,' he said, and went to the bush.

He pushed aside the leaves – and gave a cry of surprise. 'Oh – here it is – and I say – there's somebody in it! Hey, little fellow, who are you?'

The two children gazed down at their engine with its coloured trucks. In the cab of the engine was a small man with a very long beard, pointed ears and bright green eyes. His coat was as green as the leaves around.

The little fellow looked up at them in surprise and then leapt off the engine. He dived under the bush – but Robin dived after him! Betty gave a loud squeal.

'Oh, what is it – who is it – what's he doing here?'

Robin came out of the bush, his face red with excitement. In his hand he held the little green-coated man, who was wriggling and shouting.

8

'Put me down! Let me go! I wasn't doing any harm!'

Robin stood him gently on a garden-seat, still holding him. The rain had stopped, and the sun suddenly came out, so that all the garden was a-sparkle with raindrops hanging on the leaves. There seemed to be magic in the air!

9

'Who are you?' asked Robin. 'And what are you doing with our engine?'

'I didn't know it was yours,' said the little fellow, his eyes shining very green. 'I'm Run-About the brownie, and I live in Brownie-Town.'

'Why, goodness me – isn't that Fairyland?' said Betty, excited.

'Well, it's part of Fairyland,' said Run-About. 'The nicest part, we brownies think. Now, do please let me go.'

'Not yet,' said Robin. 'What were you doing with our engine?'

'Well, you see, I'm a messenger that's why I'm called Run-About,' said the brownie, 'and I was told to take a message to the squirrel who lives in your garden. It's a long way here and I was tired – and when I saw your lovely engine lying here all alone, I thought I could use it to take me back to Brownie-Town.'

'But it doesn't go by itself, silly!' said Betty, laughing.

'I know. But I can make it go all right,' said Run-About. 'I always carry quite a lot of magic with me.'

Betty and Robin felt so excited that they

hardly knew what to do next! Why, this little man might have come straight out of their story-books! Were they dreaming? No – two people couldn't have the same dream. It was real.

'Let's take him into our playroom,' said Robin. 'I'd like to ask him a lot of questions!'

'Yes, let's,' said Betty. 'We'll leave the engine here now it's stopped raining, and fetch it afterwards. Come on, Robin – bring little Run-About.'

'You will let me go, won't you?' said Run-About, as they went indoors, Robin carrying the little brownie gently in his hand.

'Yes, we will. But it *is* so exciting to meet someone like you,' said Robin. 'We can't let you go just yet! You come and see all our toys!'

They were soon in the playroom, and then Robin put the small man down on the floor. Door and windows were shut, so he couldn't run away!

Run-About gazed round in surprise. 'Oh, what a lovely place! Oh, look at that little house – why it would just be big enough for me!'

'It's my doll's house,' said Betty. 'You can open the front door and go inside, if you like!'

11

ha! ha!

But the little man had now caught sight of Robin's clockwork car, and he ran over to it in excitement. 'A little car! Just my size, too!'

He was so pleased and excited about everything in the playroom that Robin couldn't help laughing.

'Oh, what a lovely tea-set!' said Run-About, when he saw Betty's doll's tea-set. 'And oh – *look* at this magnificent aeroplane – and

12

here's a boat! What a lovely place this is! Can I come and visit it whenever I like?'

'Yes,' said Robin, pleased. 'But Run-About – can we visit you too? Please say yes!'

'Of course!' said Run-About. 'I'll take you to my home straightaway – if you'll let me drive that wooden engine of yours!'

'Come on, then!' said Robin, in excitement. 'Let's go out into the garden again and find the engine. Quick, Betty, come along. Oh, what an adventure this will be!'

Fantastic

Chapter 2

A Little Bit of Magic

Robin, Betty and Run-About the brownie ran out into the garden. The brownie ran as quickly as a little mouse. They came to the wooden engine and trucks, lying where they had left them.

The rain had quite stopped now, and the sun was hot. 'I'm too warm in my mac and sou'wester,' said Robin. 'Put them in the shed, Betty.'

Betty ran with them to the shed. The small brownie got into the cab of the engine, smiling all over his face.

'How can *we* get in?' asked Robin. 'We're too big.'

'Easy!' called back the brownie. 'I'll make you small! Put your foot into one of the

14

trucks – you too, Betty – and shut your eyes. Quick, now!'

Each of the children put their toe into a truck, and shut their eyes. A big wind suddenly blew – and they gasped, their breath taken away. They opened their eyes.

Goodness me, what had happened in that moment? 'We've gone small!' cried Robin. 'We're small enough to get into a truck! How did you do it, brownie?'

'I felt just as if I was going right down in a lift!' said Betty, sounding out of breath. 'You did some real magic then, didn't you, Run-About?'

'Yes. I told you I always carried some about with me,' said the brownie. He hopped out of the engine and bent down to its wheels. Robin looked out of his truck to see what he was doing.

'I'm rubbing a bit of Get-Along Magic into the wheels,' said Run-About. 'That's all this engine wants to make it go!'

He climbed back into the cab and beamed round at the children. The engine had two trucks, and Robin was in the first one, Betty in the second.

'All ready?' he asked. 'How does it feel to be small like me?'

15

'Nice,' said Betty. 'But oh dear, the bushes seem *enormous* and those daisies over there look so big that I could sit quite comfortably on their yellow middles! Ooooh – what's that?'

'It's a butterfly,' said Run-About, cheerfully. 'A peacock butterfly, that's all! Looking for honey, I expect.'

'It's as big as an eagle to us!' said Robin, as the pretty thing flew over them. 'Let's go, Run-About. I do want to find out how you get into Fairyland from here!'

'Well, there are entrances in all kinds of places,' said Run-About. 'Sometimes a hollow tree leads to Fairyland, sometimes a rabbit-hole, sometimes a cave in a hillside. But not many people know these. I know most of them, of course.'

The wooden engine suddenly began to creak and groan. 'We're off!' said Run-About, pleased. 'The magic is working in the wheels. Hold tight!'

The wooden wheels of the engine suddenly began to turn and off went the little train, making a rattling noise.

It ran out from under the bush, over the grass, and on to the path that went to the bottom of the garden.

'Oh – there's the gardener!' said Robin. 'Quick, he mustn't see us!'

But it was too late. The engine and trucks rattled past his legs, and he gave a yell of surprise.

'Hey – what's this!

17

Robin and Betty laughed and laughed as they rattled past him. They went right down the path to the hedge at the foot of the garden, and through a gap there into the field beyond.

'Hold tight now,' said Run-About, 'we're going down a rabbit-hole, and we'll be in the dark for a bit. Hold tight!'

They held on tightly to the sides of the trucks as the engine shot down a big rabbit-hole. Well, well — to think that one of the entrances to Fairyland was so very near their own garden! Who would have thought it!

It was quite dark in the rabbit-hole, and the children could see nothing at all. Suddenly they stopped at a wide place in the burrow, and saw two gleaming eyes looking at them. Then something soft brushed past them, and they went on once more.

'That was a rabbit,' explained Run-About. 'We waited at a passing-place so that he could get by. I expect you saw his eyes.'

'Yes, I did. I wondered what they were, they looked so enormous!' said Robin. 'Run-About, is everyone in Fairyland as small as you?'

'Pretty well — except for a giant or two,'

said Run-About. 'But you needn't worry about them – we only keep good ones in Fairyland! Ah – here we are – the other end of the tunnel!'

The engine ran out into daylight, and the sun suddenly shone down again on Robin and Betty. They gazed round in delight. Everything seemed the right size now. Trees grew here and there, and fields lay around,

gleaming with flowers that the children didn't know.

Then Robin saw a peculiar tree – it really and truly looked as if it had biscuits growing on it instead of flowers!

'Stop, Run-About,' he said. 'I want to look at that tree. It makes me feel hungry!'

'Oh, that?' said Run-About. 'Yes, it's a biscuit tree. Do hop out and pick a pocketful – they're most delicious!'

Dear me – *what* a lovely land to come to!

Chapter 3

To Brownie-Town

It was very exciting to pick biscuits off a tree. Robin and Betty picked quite a lot and then went back to the train. Robin nibbled one.

'Oh – it's _lovely_!' he said. 'It tastes of honey.'

'Of course,' said Run-About. 'It's a Honey Biscuit Tree. And over there is a Chocolate Biscuit Tree, look. And we'll soon be passing a Sausage Roll Bush – most useful if you happen to be late for dinner. But we mustn't stop any more.'

The engine started off again, rattling along well, keeping to paths or roads, and pulling its two trucks easily.

Run-About was very proud to be driving it.

All the people they met stared in wonder at him, and he felt very important indeed.

The children sat in the trucks and munched the delicious honey biscuits, looking at everything they passed. They went through a most exciting market, where little folk of all kinds bought and sold.

'A fairy with wings, look!' said Betty. 'And more brownies like Run-About. And that must be a wizard. Robin ½ see his pointed hat and flying cloak!'

Pixies, elves, brownies, imps, gnomes – all the many folk of Fairyland were there. And the buildings were as interesting as the people!

'Look at that tower reaching right up into the clouds!' said Robin. 'And surely that glittering place over there must be a palace?'

'Yes. It belongs to Prince Bong,' said Run-About. 'It has fifty thousand windows, that's why it glitters. And that's the castle belonging to Wizard Hoo-Ha over there. Once it disappeared when a spell he was making went wrong – we were all *so* surprised. But it came back the next day.'

'This must be a very, very exciting place to live in,' said Betty. 'Oh, look at those dear little crooked cottages!'

Well done

'Do you like them?' said Run-About. 'Mine is just the same. We'll soon be in Brownie-Town and I'll show you my own dear little cottage.'

They ran into a small town with curious little shops and houses. Run-About stopped at the very end. The children looked at the cottage there.

'Oh – it's *lovely*!' said Betty. 'Such funny chimneys! And a thatched roof. But there's no door, Run-About!'

'No. I have two doors, really, but when I go off on one of my journeys, I make a spell to turn them into part of the wall,' said Run-About. 'Then nobody can get in. I keep losing my keys, you see, but now I don't mind about keys – I just use a spell.'

He jumped out, and took a pencil from his pocket. He drew a rather crooked outline of a door in the front wall, and a knocker on it. He knocked loudly – and hey presto, his pencilled door became a real one – just as crooked as he had drawn it!

The children went inside. What a dear little place! Run-About went to a cupboard and opened it. Inside, on the shelves, were pies and cakes and tarts and biscuits – all kinds of delicious-looking things!

'Choose what you like and we'll sit down and have a talk,' said Run-About. So soon they were sitting in funny little chairs, eating and talking as fast as they could.

'I told you I was a messenger,' said Run-

About, eating a big jam tart. 'When anything goes wrong in Fairyland, a message is sent to me, and I have to go off to try and put it right. I mean – suppose a bridge breaks down, the message comes to me – and off I go to find someone to mend the bridge. I'm always running about all over the place – that's how I get my name, as I told you.'

'Have you been very busy lately?' asked Robin, taking a bun full of cream.

'Very,' said the brownie. 'Too busy. I've been told to take a holiday. If I get too tired I can't do any magic, you see – then I'm not much use in Fairyland.'

'Run-About – come and stay with *us* for a holiday!' cried Betty, suddenly. 'Do, please do! You can live in our playroom, with all our toys. You'd love that. And we'd play with you whenever we can. It would be a fine holiday for you!'

'Well – that's quite an idea!' said Run-About, his green eyes shining. 'I think I will! But I'd have to leave my address with somebody in case I was wanted. Something might happen that only I could put right.'

'Well, leave *our* address,' said Robin. 'Haven't you got anyone who would come with a letter to you, if things went wrong?'

'Yes. Plenty of creatures would help,' said Run-About. 'Mice or birds or even rabbits could be sent with a message. Yes – I'd love to come for a holiday with you!'

And that is how it came about that Run-About went to have a holiday with Robin and Betty, and how they came to share in many strange adventures. I really must tell you all about them.

Now – there they go, back to the playroom in the children's house, rattling along in the wooden train – but this time Robin is in the cab with Run-About, and Betty is in the first truck, waiting for *her* turn to get into the cab. You don't know what exciting things are going to happen, Robin and Betty. What fun you're going to have!

Chapter 4

A Message for Run-About

It was very exciting to have a brownie living in the playroom! Nobody but Robin and Betty knew he was there, of course. He was very happy indeed, and lived in the doll's house most of the time.

'The biggest bed just fits me,' he said. 'And I do love cooking on the little kitchen stove. Do you mind if I clean the house properly? It's rather dirty and dusty, and the curtains could do with a wash.'

'Oh *yes* – please do,' said Betty. 'It's so difficult for me to clean all the little things there with my big hands! You *are* kind, Run-About. I do so love to see you popping in and out of the front door, and waving to us from the windows!'

Run-About played with all the toys, of course, and longed and longed to sail in the boat. So one night Robin smuggled him into the bathroom when he was having his bath, and Run-About bobbed up and down in the boat very happily.

'Make bigger waves!' he said. 'Bigger ones still! That's right – it's just like the real sea!'

He told the children all kinds of curious

tales – stories of witches and wizards, and spells and enchantments. He really was a most interesting visitor to have!'

'I *am* enjoying this holiday!' he said. 'Especially as nobody has been to bother me about anything. Thank goodness nothing seems to have gone wrong in Fairyland lately!'

It was funny he should say that, because that very afternoon a message came for him. It was brought by a robin. He came flying down to the window-sill with a piece of paper in his beak.

'It's for me,' said Run-About. 'Bother! I hope I haven't to go back home.' He took the paper from the robin and read it.

'Oh dear – yes, something must be done about this. The little arched bridge over the stream near Brownie-Town has broken – and it *must* be mended before midnight because Prince Bong is coming back to his castle tomorrow – he's been away visiting his brother Bing.'

'But – how can you possibly mend a bridge before midnight?' said Robin. 'It would take our workmen *weeks* to do!'

'I'll have to think,' said Run-About, and he

went into the doll's house and sat down on the little stool there, thinking hard.

He jumped up at last and came running out of the little front door. 'I've got it! I can easily mend the bridge if you'll lend me your Meccano set – you know, that collection of bits and pieces that you build things with. You made a lovely crane the other day.'

'Oh yes – of course we'll lend it to you,' said Robin. 'On one condition! That we come and see you mend the bridge!'

'Right!' said Run-About, beaming. 'Come on – we'll go in the engine. Take it into the garden, and bring the box of Meccano things. Don't let anyone see us!'

It wasn't long before they were all speeding away in the wooden train again! Robin and Betty were as small as before, and very excited. The Meccano box was in the last truck.

Down the garden, through the gap in the hedge and down the rabbit-hole! Rattle-rattle, rumble-rumble – that wooden train could certainly go fast when it had Get-Along magic in its wheels! It ran out of the rabbit-hole at last and there they all were in Fairyland again. How lovely!

'We'll go to Brownie-Town and find the broken bridge,' said Run-About. 'No – we can't stop at that biscuit tree – sorry. We'll do our work first and play and eat afterwards!'

They came to the little stream and followed the road beside it. But when they came to the bridge that went over it to the

other side, they could get no further – the bridge was quite broken! It had sagged in the middle, and now it was too dangerous for anything to travel over it.

Two brownies were there, very pleased to see Run-About. 'You're our only hope!' they said. 'You and your good ideas! We've only got till midnight to mend the bridge, Run-About.'

'Whatever happened?' said the brownie.

'One of the giants came along and stupidly walked over the bridge,' said a brownie. 'Crash! That was the end of it – and will you believe it, the giant grumbled because his foot had gone into the water and had got wet!'

'Those giants!' said Run-About, crossly. 'Well it's *quite* impossible to mend the bridge, I'm afraid – but I've a much better idea.'

'What?' asked the two brownies.

'These children have lent me a wonderful box of bits and pieces,' said Run-About, and he showed them the box of Meccano. 'It would be easier to build a fine new bridge than to mend the old one.'

'What a fine idea!' said the brownies, and

soon all the things were being emptied out of the big box. They seemed enormous to the children now, because they themselves were so small!

'Now!' said Run-About, rolling up his sleeves. 'To work, everyone! We've *got* to build a bridge as fast as ever we can!'

Chapter 5

A Fine Little Bridge

It was great fun to build a Meccano bridge over the little river. Robin took charge, because he had so often built all kinds of things in the playroom – cranes and bridges, signals, towers and goodness knows what!

The brownies were very sharp, and did exactly what Robin told them. Betty just handed the pieces one to the other, because she wasn't really very good at building and fixing things together.

'It's a good thing the pieces are so light,' she said. 'I hope they'll be strong enough for a bridge!'

'Oh yes!' said Run-About. 'Anyway I can always add a Hold-Up spell if we're not sure. Does this piece fasten here, Robin?'

'Yes, that's right. I say, we *are* getting on,' said Robin, pleased. 'Shall we make half this side, and then go to the other side and make the other half there – and fit the middles together afterwards!'

'Good idea!' said Run-About. So they made half the bridge, one side of the river, and then Run-About borrowed a tiny boat and they all rowed off to the other side.

Betty's job was to row backwards and forwards fetching the pieces they wanted. She worked very hard indeed!

Soon the other half of the bridge was built, and the two halves met in the middle. Robin very carefully joined them together – and the bridge was finished! It really was a fine one.

The children and the brownies looked at it proudly. 'Couldn't be better,' said Run-About, running to and fro over it. 'As strong as you like! It doesn't even need a Hold-Up spell!'

'I wish we could see Prince Bong's carriage coming across tonight!' said Betty.

'Well – we'll see,' said Run-About. He turned to the other two brownies. 'Send a message to Prince Bong that a new bridge has been built for him. I'm going on holiday again!'

Off the three of them went in the little wooden train – and this time they stopped at the Chocolate Biscuit Tree and also at a tree they hadn't seen before, which grew jam tarts just like big open flowers!

'I wish we grew trees like this in our world,' said Betty. 'Why don't we!'

They were all very tired that evening, and the children went to sleep quickly, wondering whether Run-About would wake them to see Prince Bong going over the bridge they had built for him!

But Run-Around was fast asleep too, and it really looked as if nobody would wake up at all!

And then a tapping came at the playroom window – tap-tap-tap – tap! Tap-tap-tap!

Run-About awoke at once, ran out of the doll's house and went to the window.

'Run-About? I've a message for you,' said a small high voice, and a tiny pixie looked in. 'The Princess Goldie was flying home from a dance tonight on her bat, and he stupidly got caught in the topmost branches of a tree – in your world here, too! She sent a message for you to go and help. Whatever can you do?'

'Goodness! *I* don't know!' said Run-About, astonished. 'Wait – I'll go and wake two children here and see if they have any good ideas.'

Then Robin suddenly felt his shoulder tapped and woke up with a jump to hear Run-About's voice by his ear. The little fellow was up on his pillow.

'Robin! A messenger has come to me. The Princess Goldie is in trouble. Listen!'

He told the boy all about it, and Robin got out of bed to wake Betty. Soon the three of them were having a little meeting.

'How can we get to the top of a big tree in the darkness, and rescue the Princess and take her home?' said Run-About. 'This is the biggest puzzle I've ever had!'

'Run-About – I suppose you couldn't make our toy aeroplane fly, could you?' said Betty, suddenly.

'Of course! The very thing!' cried Run-About. 'I've often wanted to fly in that lovely little aeroplane. I've got plenty of Fly-High magic. I'll go and get it. You get the aeroplane!'

Well, it wasn't long before Robin, Betty, the pixie at the window, and Run-About were all in the aeroplane, the children made as small as the others! They were on the window-sill by the open window, ready to take off.

Run-About had rubbed a Fly-High spell on the wings of the plane, and they were beginning to make a curious humming noise. They quivered and shook – and then, with a swoop, the aeroplane was off into the night-sky, flying beautifully.

'Oh, how wonderful!' cried Betty, looking down at the moonlit world beneath her. 'Oh, what a fine feeling it is to fly high like this!'

'Guide us to the tree where the Princess Goldie waits with her bat,' said Run-About to the pixie. 'We'll soon be there!'

How that toy aeroplane flew – really, it was the most exciting thing that had ever happened to the two children!

Chapter 6

A Most Exciting Night

It was quite a long way to the big tree, but at last the aeroplane arrived there. It circled over the very top, and Run-About looked down in the bright moonlight.

A small voice called out. 'Oh, what's this? An aeroplane! Who is in it, please?'

'Me, Your Highness – Run-About the Brownie,' called Run-About. 'I got your message. I'll get the aeroplane to hover like a butterfly just over your branch – and if you stand up, we'll pull you in. Ready?'

The aeroplane hovered just over the bough where the Princess stood, and she stretched out her arms. Run-About and Robin pulled her gently up and into the aeroplane!

She was the prettiest little thing Robin and Betty had ever seen. 'Like one of the pictures in our fairytale books!' whispered Robin to Betty.

'It's very kind of you to fetch me like this,' said the Princess. 'I really didn't know *what* to do! My bat hurt his wing when he flew into the tree – a most extraordinary thing for a bat to do, but I think he must have been very sleepy. I've bound up his wing and it will be better tomorrow. He's crept under a bough and hung himself upside down to sleep.'

'We'll soon take you back to your castle, dear Princess,' said Run-About. Robin gave him a nudge and whispered to him.

'Do we pass anywhere near the Meccano bridge we built?' he said. 'I do so want to see Prince Bong going over it with his carriage!'

'Ah, yes,' said Run-About, remembering. He turned to the princess. 'Your Highness,' he said, 'would you like to see a marvellous new bridge I and some friends built today? I can easily hover over it.'

'Yes, I would!' said the Princess Goldie. 'Somebody told me about it. It sounds grand!'

'Look – what's that down there?' suddenly said Betty, looking over the side of the aeroplane.

'It's Prince Bong's carriage on the road home!' said Run-About. 'Good! We'll follow him and watch him use our bridge!'

So, in great excitement they flew above the galloping horses and the shining carriage in which they saw Prince Bong.

'I can see the river – we're coming to it!'

cried Betty. 'Oh Robin – suppose our bridge wasn't strong enough and broke just when Prince Bong drove over it. Whatever should we do?'

Everyone began to feel rather worried. The carriage was drawn by eight horses, and looked rather solid and heavy. Surely the little light bridge they had made would not hold the carriage and horses when they drove right across. Why, oh why, hadn't Run-About put a Hold-Up spell on the pieces?

The horses galloped towards the bridge. The coachman slowed down a little as he came near.

'It's just a bit narrow,' said Robin, watching. 'Ah – there goes the first pair of horses on the new bridge!'

The first pair was followed by the second, and soon all the horses, and the carriage too, were on the bridge. Everyone in the aeroplane held their breath. What a load was on that little bridge!

But the bridge held! It creaked just a little when the carriage rolled on, but it held! It really was very well made, and Robin couldn't help feeling proud.

'It's one thing to build a *toy* bridge,' he

said to Betty, 'but this one is a *real* bridge, meant to be used. Run-About, are you pleased?'

Run-About's green eyes shone brightly, and he nodded his head.

'Rather!' he said. 'Well, we've been very busy today and tonight, haven't we? Making a bridge, and rescuing Princess Goldie! We'd better get on now, and fly to her castle.'

Off went the aeroplane again, its little propeller whirring madly. Robin leaned back in his seat. Who would have thought that he would ever ride in his own toy aeroplane? It was really too good to be true!

'There's my castle,' said Princess Goldie, pointing over the side of the aeroplane. Everyone looked down to see it.

It rose up high on a hill, quite a small castle, but a beautiful one, with towers soaring high.

'It's got a drawbridge!' said Robin. 'I've always longed to have a drawbridge let down for me!'

'Well, you shall,' said the Princess. 'I want you to come in and have supper with me. I haven't had much to eat at the dance and I'm hungry.'

So, to Robin's great delight, when the aeroplane flew down beside the great moat that circled the castle, the drawbridge was let down for him to walk over.

'You go first,' said the Princess, 'and feel as grand as you like, Robin!'

So Robin walked over the drawbridge, feeling really very important indeed, and the others followed. Then, with a creak and a groan the drawbridge was drawn up again into place. Now no one could go in or out!

What a wonderful supper they had – and dear me, what did Robin and Betty do afterwards but fall fast asleep! Run-About laughed to see them.

'We'll never get them into the aeroplane again tonight!' he said. 'They must sleep here.'

But what would their mother say when she went into their bedroom next morning and found them missing? What a to-do there would be! Wake up, Robin, wake up, Betty, but no, they won't even open their eyes!

Chapter 7

The Little Roundabout Man

When Robin and Betty woke up next day they remembered all that had happened the night before. They had walked over the drawbridge into Princess Goldie's castle, they had had a wonderful supper with her – and then they had fallen asleep!

'We must be in the castle still – how exciting!' said Robin, and he opened his eyes.

But they weren't in the castle! They were in their beds at home. Robin sat up in surprise. 'But we *can't* be at home – we didn't get back into the aeroplane, I know!'

He ran into the playroom to see if the toy aeroplane was back. No, it wasn't. And Run-About wasn't there either! How

49

strange. Then how did he and Betty get back?

He went to talk to Betty and she couldn't understand it either. They had their breakfast and then went back to the playroom, feeling very puzzled.

Suddenly a whirring noise came to their ears – and in at the window flew the little toy aeroplane, shining in the sun! It landed on the floor very neatly and out jumped Run-About, grinning all over his little bearded face.

'Hello!' he said. 'I'm back again. I stayed the night in the castle and flew home after breakfast.'

The children stared at him in surprise. 'Well, then – how did *we* get back here?' asked Betty. 'We didn't come in the aeroplane!'

'No. The Princess Goldie knew a very clever spell,' said Run-About. 'She rubbed a spell on your eyes to make you wake up in your own beds – and you did.'

'But – but I still don't understand how we got here,' said Robin, puzzled.

'Magic never *can* be understood,' said Run-About. 'So don't worry about it. Didn't we have an exciting time last night? I'm getting quite famous in Fairyland now, what with making bridges and flying aeroplanes!'

'Oh – then perhaps *another* message will be sent to you soon, to put something else right,' said Betty, pleased. 'I must say you're an exciting visitor to have, Run-About!'

'I wonder what your next message will be,' said Robin.

He didn't have very long to wonder. When they were out in the garden after tea, playing hide-and-seek, a little red squirrel sat up in a tree, watching. Robin saw him and pointed him out to Betty and Run-About.

'Why – he's come to give me some news, I'm sure!' said Run-About. 'It's Frisky, from Brownie-Town!' He beckoned to the squirrel, who bounded down at once.

The squirrel whispered into Run-About's ear. 'Dear, dear,' said Run-About, looking all round. 'Where is he? Tell him he can come out of his hiding-place, these children are my friends.'

Then, to the children's surprise, from out of a clump of snapdragons came a funny little fellow, his hat in his hand. He bowed low to Run-About.

'Sir,' he said, 'I have heard of your fame, and how you built that wonderful bridge. People say you can do anything! So I have come to ask your help.'

The children gazed at this funny little man, no bigger than Run-About. He was dressed in very gay clothes, and his hat had an enormously long feather in it.

'Who are you?' asked Run-About, looking pleased.

'I am Mr Heyho, the Roundabout Man, from the great Fair in Pixie Village,' said the little man. 'A dreadful thing has happened, sir.'

'What is it?' asked Run-About.

'A witch complained of the noise that my roundabout music made,' said Mr Heyho, 'and when I told her that I couldn't stop my roundabout just to please her, she was very angry. She flew over it on her broomstick and dropped a spell into the machinery that makes it work . . .'

'And now I suppose it won't go round and round any more!' said Run-About.

'You're right,' said Mr Heyho. 'And I'm losing a lot of money, Mr Run-About, and the owner of the Fair, Mr Stamp-Around, says I'll have to take my roundabout away and he'll get another.'

'Ah – I know old Stamp-Around,' said Run-About. 'A very hot-tempered fellow. Well, what do you expect me to do, Heyho?'

'I don't know, sir,' said Heyho. 'The witch's spell won't wear off for three days, I'm afraid. I thought perhaps you'd go and ask her to remove it.'

'Good gracious! I wouldn't go near a witch

for anything!' said Run-About. 'I'm afraid I can't help you, Heyho.'

'Couldn't you even find me a new round-about for three days?' said Heyho, dolefully.

Run-About shook his head. 'You can't buy roundabouts easily!' he said. 'No – I'm sorry, but this time I can't do anything to help!'

Heyho turned to go, looking very sad. But before he had disappeared, Betty called out to him.

'Wait! Wait a minute! I've thought of someting that might do. Something in the playroom.'

'What do you mean? *We* haven't a round-about,' said Robin.

'Come up to the playroom and I'll show you something I think will do!' said Betty.

And there they all go at top speed. Whatever in the world has Betty thought of?

Chapter 8

What a Peculiar Roundabout!

Soon Robin and Betty were in the play-room with Run-About and little Mr Heyho. Robin was puzzled. What *had* Betty got in her mind? He knew quite well that there was nothing at all like a roundabout among their toys.

Betty went to the cupboard and rummaged at the back. She brought out a great big humming-top! She put it down with its pointed end to the floor, and began to work the handle up and down that spun it.

Soon the great top was spinning all over the playroom floor, humming as loudly as a hundred bees! Heyho stared at it in the greatest delight.

'Why – that's a perfect roundabout – with its own lovely humming music too!'

'Yes. That's what I thought,' said Betty, pleased. 'Do you think you could use it for a roundabout at your Fair till the witch's spell has worn off your own?'

'Yes – certainly I could!' said Heyho. 'But how could I spin it to make it go round? I'm not big or strong enough.'

'I'll put a Spin Spell into it,' said Run-About. 'Then it will spin itself whenever you say "Spin, top, spin!"'

'Oh – thank you very much,' said Heyho, delighted. 'Can we take it now? How can we get it to the Fair?'

'We could take it in the wooden engine,' said Robin. 'In the second truck. Come on – let's all go. I'll have a ride on the Humming-Top Roundabout too!'

'I say! What fun!' said Betty, thrilled. 'Can we do anything else, Mr Heyho?'

'You can do anything you like,' said Heyho, so happy that he was full of smiles. 'You can go on the swings and down the slippery-slip and throw hoopla rings to see if you can get a prize, and have a go at the coconut shy, and . . .'

'Oh quick, I can't wait! Do come along!' cried Betty. 'Where's the engine? Engine, we're off to Fairyland again!'

And soon away they went as usual, carrying the big top in the second truck. Betty stood in the first truck, as soon as she had been made small enough, and held the top steady, because it rolled round and round in the truck, and she was afraid it might be bumped out, and lost down the rabbit-hole.

It didn't take them very long to arrive at the Fair. It really was a fine one! There was a row of swings that went to and fro and up and down. There was a long and winding slippery-slip packed with squealing pixies. There was a coconut shy where many brownies were throwing balls at rows of coconuts standing on pegs.

And there was the roundabout, of course, but it stood still and silent. No music came from it, and no movement. All round it stood the little folk, looking very sad because they couldn't have a ride on the lovely roundabout.

A man came stamping up, looking very cross. It was the owner of the Fair, Mr Stamp-Around.

'Hey, there!' he called. 'You've got to remove that roundabout. I want to put something else there. It's no use at all, that roundabout of yours, Heyho.'

'I've found the very newest kind of roundabout there is!' shouted back Heyho. 'It makes its own music – and sounds like a hundred bees!'

He and Run-About stood the great humming-top on its foot. Run-About rubbed a powerful spell all round it.

> *'Now begin*
> *To spin, top, spin,*
> *Go round and round,*
> *With humming sound,*
> *And tumble people on the ground!'*

The children heard him whispering this rhyme as he rubbed his magic on to the top. A low humming sound began to come from it.

'Climb up and hold on! The new roundabout is about to spin!' cried Heyho. 'A penny a spin! Only a penny!'

Soon the top was crowded with dozens of little folk, all laughing and chattering. What a peculiar roundabout!

'Spin, top, spin!' said Heyho – and at once the great top began to spin round and round, slowly at first, and then faster and faster! It hummed louder still, and an old woman nearby looked round and about, expecting to see a swarm of bees. But it was only the top humming!

What fun it was! And when the top slowed down, sending all the little folk rolling on the ground, how they laughed and shouted.

'It's a grand roundabout!' they said. 'Let's go on it again!'

But this time Betty, Robin and Run-About were the only ones allowed on. How Betty squealed when the top went faster and faster, and filled her ears with its humming!

They all enjoyed it very much, and tumbled off happily when the top slowed down and rolled over. 'Now let's try the other things!' said Robin.

And off they went to swing on the swings, and slide down the winding slippery-slip, and throw the wooden balls at the coconuts. Robin won a big one, and so did Run-About. Betty threw a hoop at the hoopla stall, and it fell exactly round a lovely little brooch. The hoopla man pinned it on her dress. She was so pleased.

They didn't want to leave the exciting Fair but they dared not be late for their dinner. What would they say if Mummy asked them where they had been that morning? She would never believe them if they told her that they had taken their humming-top to a Fair and made it into a roundabout!

'You are a most exciting friend to have, Run-About,' said Robin, as they went back in the little wooden train. 'I do wonder what will happen next?'

Chapter 9

Tiptoe Tells Her Tale

For two days nothing happened at all, and the children were quite disappointed. Then somebody came to see Run-About, someone who looked most upset.

It was a pretty little pixie looking rather like the fairy doll who always stood at the top of the children's tree each Christmas. Run-About knew her at once, when she flew down into the playroom, where he was watching the children build with bricks.

He jumped up quickly. 'Oh – Tiptoe! What's the matter? You're crying!'

The children looked at the pretty little thing and wished their hankies were small enough to wipe her eyes. She rubbed away her tears and tried to smile.

'Oh, Run-About – I'm sorry, to burst in like this, but it's very, very urgent.'

'Tell me,' said Run-About. 'Nothing has happened to your sisters, has it?'

'Yes. Something dreadful!' said Tiptoe. 'I was out shopping today when the Enchanter Frown-Hard came along to our cottage and saw my sisters playing in the garden. And he's captured them all and taken them away!'

'How shocking!' said Run-About, in dismay. 'They'll be so frightened. Where has he taken them?'

'To the tower that reaches the clouds,' said Tiptoe. 'You know the one, don't you – its tip goes right up to the highest clouds. And he's going to keep them prisoners there just because the ball they were playing with hit him on his horrid long nose!'

'We must rescue them,' said Run-About at once.

'But how, dear Run-About?' said Tiptoe. 'We can't get into the tower, because he has taken the door away by magic – it's just brick wall all round.'

'I'll put another one there,' said Tiptoe, valiantly.

'But listen – after Frown-Hard had sent them all up to the very top of the tower, he made the *stairs* disappear too,' said Tiptoe, beginning to cry again. 'So it's just no good trying to get into the tower.'

'The aeroplane!' suddenly said Betty. 'Couldn't we fly to the top of the tower in that and rescue them?'

'No. The Enchanter thought of that,' said Tiptoe, sadly. 'He's got someone watching out for aeroplanes. He's already caught one, with my uncle in it. Oh dear – what are we to do?'

'Perhaps he wouldn't see an aeroplane at night?' said Betty. 'Could we go then, do you think?'

'No. He'd hear it,' said Tiptoe. Then she suddenly smiled. 'Oh! *I* know! I know something that would fly to the top of the tower without a sound!'

'Who? What?' cried Run-About, excited.

'A kite!' said Tiptoe. 'A kite on a very long string. Have these children got a kite? Oh, do say yes!'

They had, of course, and they at once went to their toy cupboard to find it. They pulled it out – a big flat kite with a smiling face and a long tail made of newspaper screwed up into pieces.

'Here it is,' said Betty, pleased. 'But Run-About, you mustn't make this kite small when you get to Fairyland, or it would never take all Tiptoe's sisters! And how are they to come down on it? They would tumble off.'

'Easy,' said Run-About, 'the kite must fly higher than the tower, and flap its long tail against the top window. Then each little sister can climb out and hang on to a bit of the tail! Then off the kite flies to our land!'

'Oh *yes!*' said Tiptoe. 'Let's send a bee to hum the news to my sisters. The Enchanter would never notice such a small creature at the top of the tower!'

'We must wait till the evening,' said Run-About. 'It's no good flying a kite in the daytime – it would certainly be seen.'

It was hard to wait so long, and Tiptoe sighed all day, thinking of her small scared sisters. They sent a message by a big bumblebee and he came back to say that he had told the little pixies the news, and they would be sure to look out for the kite that night.

Once more the children and Run-About set off in the wooden engine. It was difficult to take the big kite down the rabbit-hole, so Run-About went a different way. He took them through a cave in a distant hill – and hey presto, when they came out of the big tunnel in the hill, they found themselves not far from the Meccano bridge that they had built over the river.

'It's still there!' said Robin, in delight. 'Let's drive over it in the engine.'

So they trundled over the bridge they had built, and it didn't even shake! Then on they went till they came to the Enchanter's castle, gleaming in the moonlight.

Some distance away was the high tower, soaring right up to the clouds. Goodness, how tall it was! But the kite wouldn't mind that – it liked flying high!

Run-About had a very big ball of string. He would need a lot if the kite was to fly as high as the clouds!

The wind blew a little and the kite tried to get out of the truck. 'All right – be patient – you're soon going to fly!' said Run-About. 'We'd better be very, very quiet now, everyone!'

The kite was taken from the truck. It seemed very big to the children now, because, as usual, they had gone small as soon as they got into the train. It took all four of them to pull the kite into position so that the wind could take it.

'We'd better all of us hang on to the string,' said Run-About. 'My word – there it goes up into the air. Fly to the topmost window of the tower, kite – that's right – higher and higher – you're nearly there!'

Chapter 10

What an Exciting Time!

The kite rose high in the wind, and tugged so hard at the string that the children and Run-About were almost jerked off their feet. Little Tiptoe was pulled a few feet into the air, but Betty just dragged her down in time!

The string ran quickly through their fingers as the kite rose higher and higher, and nobody dared to hold it back now. Was the kite at the topmost window yet?

Yes, it was! It had reached the clouds, and its long paper tail tapped against the topmost tower window. Someone opened it cautiously.

Then, one by one, seven tiny little people climbed out, holding on to the tail of the kite. The first one sat down on the first bit of paper, the next one sat down on the second, and so on.

'Hold tight to the string of the tail,' whispered the first little sister. 'Hold tight!'

Down below Tiptoe was waiting anxiously. She was too far away to see her sisters creeping out of the tower window – but the four down below felt each little bump as the seven sisters sat themselves on the bits of paper that made the kite's tail.

'One – two – three – four – five – six – seven – they're all out of the window now, safely on the kite's tail!' said Tiptoe. 'Pull the kite down! Then we'll have them down here with us in no time, and can escape in the wooden train!'

But oh dear, oh dear, who should come up behind them just at that very moment but the horrid old Enchanter!

'Aha!' he said. 'I've been watching your clever little trick. But it won't do, you know. I'll help you to pull down the kite – and I'll capture those seven little sisters again as soon as the kite reaches the ground. And I'll have Tiptoe as well this time!'

What a dreadful shock for everyone! But Run-About was not going to have the little pixie sisters caught again. He whipped out his knife and cut the string of the kite. At once it soared high into the air, and flew off all by itself into the sky – and it took the seven little sisters with it, hanging on its tail!

'Quick, quick! Into the train!' cried Run-About, and they all leapt in. The Enchanter was so surprised by the disappearance of the kite that he didn't even try to stop them!

Off they went through the night at top speed and didn't stop till they came into the garden again. Tiptoe was crying.

'I know my sisters have escaped from the Enchanter – but I'm sure I shall never see them again!' she sobbed.

'Don't be silly,' said Run-About. 'I rubbed a Come-Back spell on the kite before I sent it up into the air. You surely might have guessed that, Tiptoe.'

'Well, I didn't,' said Tiptoe. 'Oh, how clever you are, Run-About. When will the kite come back?'

'I've no idea,' said Run-About. 'All I know is that it *will* come back, and will bring your sisters with it.'

He took Tiptoe into the playroom with him, and she got into one of the dolls' cots with a doll, though she was sure she wouldn't go to sleep! Run-About went to the doll's house and cuddled down into bed, quite tired out.

The children went to bed too, and when Betty heard a leaf tap-tapping against her window, she quite thought it was the kite, and got up to see.

But it wasn't! It hadn't come back the next morning either, and Run-About felt quite worried. Tiptoe cried and cried, and Betty gave her two tiny hankies belonging to her dolls.

They had to go out for a walk that morning, though they didn't want to leave Run-About and Tiptoe. But Mummy said it was lovely and fine, and the wind was very fresh, and they really must go out!

And will you believe it, just as they crossed the field that led to the farm, they saw a kite tangled in a tree! Was it theirs? Could it be?

Yes – it was! How wonderful! Where were the tiny sisters? Were they hurt?

They ran to the tree and climbed up. Yes, it *was* their kite, its string wrapped round and round some twigs. It really was a business to untie it! But where in the world were Tiptoe's sisters?

Betty suddenly saw them! They were all cuddled up in an old blackbird's nest, fast asleep! How sweet they looked!

'There they are – tired out!' said Betty. 'Robin, can you take the nest gently out of its place? We could carry all the little things quite safely home in the nest!'

Robin removed the old nest gently, and carried home the sleeping pixies. Betty took the kite. 'The Come-Back spell can't have been quite strong enough!' she said. 'You *nearly* got home, kite, but not quite!'

How pleased Run-About and Tiptoe were to see the seven little sisters asleep in the nest! Run-About couldn't help laughing out loud – and that woke them up!

The children loved them. They were as frisky and lively as kittens, and did the maddest things. Tiptoe decided that for one night they would all stay in the doll's house before they went back home.

And you should have seen those tiny creatures running in and out of the front door, opening and shutting the windows, cooking on the little stove, and sitting on the little chairs!

But best of all was when Betty looked through the windows at night and saw them all cuddled up into the little beds, fast asleep. I wish *we* could have seen them too, don't you?

Chapter 11

Where is Run-About?

The children felt quite sad when Tiptoe and her seven tiny sisters went home together. Run-About took them in the little wooden train, and Robin and Betty wished they could go with them, but their Granny was coming to see them that day, so they couldn't.

'You'll come back, won't you, Run-About?' said Betty, anxiously, when he got into the cab of the engine. He nodded gaily.

'Oh yes – I haven't finished my holiday with you yet! I feel much better already. I love your doll's house, it's just right for me!'

Off they went, and the children watched them go through the gap in the hedge. 'They'll be going down the rabbit-hole now,' said Betty. 'My word – wouldn't other children love to know that there are secret ways into Fairyland all over the place – if you know where to look for them!'

'We know two already,' said Robin. 'The one down the rabbit-hole and the one through the cave in the hill.'

'Of course, some of the entrances to Fairyland are too small for us to use, unless we're lucky enough to know someone like Run-About, who knows a Go-Small spell,' said Betty. 'Look – there's Granny already!'

They ran to meet their Granny, and had a lovely day with her – but all the time they were listening for Run-About to come back. They had become very fond of the green-eyed brownie, with his long, silky beard and happy ways.

He didn't come back to dinner and he didn't come back to tea, because they looked in the doll's house to see. The wooden engine wasn't back either.

'I expect he's spending the day with Tiptoe and her sisters,' said Robin. 'They really are very sweet!'

Even when bedtime came near Run-About wasn't back. The children felt sad. 'We can't possibly go and see him,' said Robin, mournfully. 'We don't know the Go-Small spell, and if we tried to find the way through that cave in the hill by ourselves, we might lose ourselves.'

'Listen – there's an owl hooting outside,' said Betty, suddenly. 'He sounds as if he's very close. Could he be bringing a message for us, do you think?'

Robin went to the window. A large owl sat on a branch outside, his big eyes gleaming as

he waited. In his sharp curved beak was a scrap of paper. He dropped it when he saw the children, spread his soft wings and flew off silently.

'Yes – it *is* a message!' said Robin, excited. 'Oh goodness me – Granny has spotted it too. She's picking it up and reading it!'

He ran down the stairs, and Granny came in from the garden at the same time, holding the scrap of paper. She held it out to Robin.

'I was just walking round the garden in the evening sunshine, when this note dropped at my feet,' she said, sounding puzzled. 'Is it for you? It must be from one of your friends, though where it came from I really don't know. Perhaps the wind brought it!'

Robin took the note and read it. 'Yes, Granny,' he said, 'it *is* from one of our friends. Thank you. I'll just go and tell Betty.'

Off he went, and he and Betty read the note together. It was from Run-About.

Shall not be home tonight, as Tiptoe is giving a tea-party at midnight to her aunt, Lady High-and-Mighty, who is passing through her village. She is half a witch, and rides on a very fine broomstick with a handle made of gold, and bristles of pure silk! I wish you could come to the party too, but Tiptoe only has ten cups and saucers – that will be seven for her sisters, and one each for herself and for me and for her aunt! She sends her love. See you tomorrow.

Your friend, Run-About.

'Oh! I do *wish* we could go to the party too!' said Betty. 'A midnight party in Fairyland, with Tiptoe and her sisters – and a guest who is half a witch.'

'She'll come riding down on her golden broomstick!' said Robin. 'Listen – there's Mummy calling. We'd better get ready for bed at once!'

They were soon asleep – but, at just about half-past eleven there came a rattling up the garden path. Robin heard it in his sleep, and awoke suddenly. He knew that rattling noise! It was the sound made by the wheels of the little wooden train. Run-About must be back!

He sat up in bed, and soon heard the patter of tiny feet in his bedroom. 'Robin! Are you awake?' said Run-About's voice. 'I want your help. Something dreadful has happened!'

'What?' asked Robin.

'Well, you know that Tiptoe was giving a midnight party for her aunt, don't you? She had just set the table with all the cups and saucers and plates, when suddenly one leg of the table collapsed – and everything fell to the floor and was smashed!'

'Oh dear – what a pity!' said Robin.

'Yes – because there are no shops open to buy another tea-set,' said Run-About. 'So I wondered if Betty would lend us her lovely doll's tea-set, Robin – it's got twelve cups and saucers and plates, hasn't it?'

'Oh yes! Betty would love to lend it to Tiptoe for her party!' said Robin. 'Let's go and tell her.'

'And, as there are *twelve* cups and saucers, would you and Betty like to come to the party too?' said Run-About as they went into Betty's room. 'Tiptoe only had ten, so she couldn't ask you – but if we have twelve, you could come too. Please do!'

'We'll come! We'll *love* to come!' said Robin in excitement. 'Oh, *what* an adventure!'

Chapter 12

A Midnight Party

Betty was just as excited as Robin was, when she was awakened and told the news. She scrambled out of bed at once.

'I'll get the tea-set now. What a good thing nothing is broken – there are twelve of every-thing still, and a lovely teapot and milk-jug and sugar-basin. Oh, I *never* thought we could use it properly, like this! What fun to be as small as you, Run-About, and drink from my own tiny tea-set!'

'Come in your dressing-gowns,' said Run-About. 'There won't be time for you to dress.'

Betty got her tea-set out of the toy cup-board, in its big box. She took the lid off and peeped inside. How tiny the cups were – but soon they would be big enough for her to drink from, because she would be as small as a doll!

Down the stairs – into the garden where the wooden train waited. Once more they became as small as Run-About and climbed into the trucks. Betty still felt as if she were going down in a lift when the Go-Small spell worked!

Off they went at top speed, almost running over a startled hedgehog, and making two little mice squeak in fright. Down the rabbit-hole, hoping not to bump into any running rabbit, and at last out of the other end and into Fairyland itself!

'Oh! Isn't Fairyland beautiful tonight, with the moon shining down brightly?' said Betty. 'And look – that tree is bright with candles! It's like a Christmas tree. Who put the candles on it, Run-About?'

'Nobody. It *grows* candles!' said Run-About. 'If we had time to stop you could pick some. But we really must hurry. Tiptoe's aunt doesn't like to be kept waiting. I only hope she's late!'

They came to Tiptoe's cottage. She had hung it with fairy-lights and it looked very

pretty indeed. Roses and honeysuckle grew all over it, right to the crooked little chimney, and scented the air as soon as they came near.

Tiptoe was waiting at the gate. She ran to meet them, her eyes shining. 'Oh, I'm so glad you've come! And you've brought the tea-set Run-About told me of – oh, isn't it lovely! Just the right size too. We'll soon have the table laid again!'

The seven little sisters twittered round the children like small birds. It was strange to be as small now as they were!

Soon they were laying the table in Tiptoe's cottage, and the two children gazed in astonishment – for there was not a scrap of food there, but only empty dishes. Well, well, well!

'Here's our Aunt High-and-Mighty!' said Tiptoe, suddenly, running into the garden.

Robin and Betty went too. What a strange sight they saw!

A shining golden broomstick was flying high above their heads in the moonlight, and on it rode somebody in a pointed hat and a long and beautiful red cloak that flew out behind in the wind. She pointed the broomstick downwards and swooped towards the garden.

She leapt off the shining broomstick and stood it against the wall. The children stared at her curiously. So this was Tiptoe's aunt, half a witch!

She smiled round and her green eyes twinkled. 'Ha! Quite a party!' she said. 'I hope you've got a meal for me, Tiptoe. I've flown right across Fairyland tonight and I'm hungry.'

'Come in, Aunt,' said Tiptoe. 'This is Run-About the brownie – and this is Robin and Betty, two good friends of ours. Your midnight tea is ready!'

They all went into the cottage. There were not enough chairs to go round the table, so Tiptoe had put two benches at each side, and a chair at each end, one for herself and one for her aunt.

They all sat down. 'Why isn't there anything to eat?' said Robin, puzzled.

Everyone laughed except Betty.

'This is a special meal,' said Tiptoe. 'My aunt once gave me a spell for parties, and I'm using it tonight. We each wish for what we want to eat, and the empty dishes will soon be filled!'

'What a splendid idea!' said Betty, excited. It certainly was fun when they all wished one by one!

'Dewdrop cake!' said Aunt High-and-Mighty. 'Honey buns!' said Run-About. 'Treacle pudding!' said Robin. 'Chocolate ice-cream!' said Betty. 'Mystery sandwiches!' said Tiptoe, and all the seven sisters wished for curious and exciting things too!

A dish was filled by magic each time anyone wished. It really was very peculiar, but the children thought that it was quite the nicest way of getting food for a party. How they enjoyed their midnight meal!

Aunt High-and-Mighty was a most interesting person. Tiptoe said she knew a great deal of magic and had done some extraordinary things. 'Please, Aunt, do tell us a few!' she said.

So the honoured guest told some very strange and mysterious tales, and the children almost stopped eating when they heard them. How they wished that, like Tiptoe, they had an aunt who was half a witch!

Tiptoe's aunt said goodbye at last, and went to get her broomstick. She suddenly turned to the two children. 'I like you,' she said. 'You're nice children with good manners. Would you like me to take you home on my broomstick, just for a treat? Jump on, then – that's right. Hold tight, we're off!'

There they go, up in the air on the shining broomstick – *what* a thing to happen!

Chapter 13

Will Anything Else Happen?

The children sat on the broomstick handle, holding tight with their hands, too excited for words as they flew through the moonlit night. Tiptoe's aunt hummed a little magic song as they went along, and the children suddenly felt sleepy.

'Oh – I'm falling asleep – and I shall fall off the broomstick!' said Betty. 'Please, please stop!'

'I'm falling asleep too,' said Robin, in alarm, and he gave an enormous yawn. 'Please, Tiptoe's aunt, fly down to earth. I know I shall fall off!'

But Tiptoe's aunt took no notice and went on humming more and more loudly. The children's eyes closed. They let go of the

broomstick – they felt themselves falling, falling, falling – then BUMP! They arrived somewhere soft and bounced up and down.

'Goodness!' said Robin, only half awake even now, 'where am I? Oh my bed, I do believe. But – how did it happen!'

Betty had landed on her bed too, but she was too sleepy to think about it. In two seconds both the children were sound asleep, still hearing the humming noise in their dreams.

They were puzzled next day about how they fell into their beds, and even Run-About, who had arrived back in the wooden train, couldn't tell them. 'Tiptoe's aunt knows a lot of very powerful magic,' he said. 'I wouldn't worry about how you got back to your beds, your right size, too, if I were you! You were very lucky to have a broomstick ride, I can tell you! I've never had one in my life!'

'We did enjoy ourselves,' said Betty, remembering the wonderful meal. 'Oh, Run-About – I wish you knew the spell to make food-wishes come true! It would be such fun to have a party like that, and let each of our guests wish for exactly what they liked!'

'I enjoyed those Mystery sandwiches,' said Robin. 'I couldn't guess what was inside any of them, but each one was nicer than the last. I wish I had a few to eat now.'

Run-About grinned, and took them to the doll's house. Inside, on the table, was a little paper bag. He took it and went out to offer it to them. Inside were some of the Mystery sandwiches, left over from the party – but they were very, very small, of course.

'I know enough magic to make them big enough for you to eat, if you like,' he said. 'Tiptoe sent them to you.'

'Oh! How lovely!' said Robin. 'Please do make them big now – as big as you can!'

Soon they were eating the Mystery sandwiches, and puzzling their heads to try and think what was inside them.

'Sardines – egg – tomato – cream – chocolate – pineapple – peppermint – goodness, I can taste all those at once!' said Betty.

'We *have* enjoyed ourselves since you came to live with us, Run-About,' said Robin. 'Life has really been very exciting. I do hope you won't go away yet.'

'I really must go next week,' said Run-About. 'It's been a lovely holiday, I must say – though I've had to do quite a lot of jobs, haven't I – with your help, of course.'

'We've *loved* helping!' said Betty. 'It was lucky we had so many toys that were just what you wanted – the Meccano for the bridge – and the tea-set last night . . .'

'And the kite for rescuing Tiptoe's sisters from the tower,' said Robin. 'And the humming-top came in well for that roundabout.'

'And the aeroplane!' said Run-About.

'And don't forget how useful your doll's house has been to me. I've used it for a proper little holiday house! I shall be sorry to leave it next week.'

'I hope something else happens before you go back to live in Fairyland,' said Betty. 'Things will be *very* dull without you, Run-About!'

'I don't expect anything will,' said Run-About. 'There's nothing much on in Fairyland at present, except the balloon-racing on Friday.'

'Balloon-racing! What's that?' said Robin, surprised.

'Oh, it's rather amusing,' said Run-About. 'You know those lovely balloons that you can blow up? Well, we enter those for the race.'

'But – what happens? Do you just blow about?' asked Betty.

'Well, when they're blown up nice and big, we fix a little basket under each one, and the racers each get into them,' said Run-About. 'Then they all set off at a given moment, and see who can go the furthest before the balloon goes flat, or drifts to earth.'

'It sounds wonderful!' said Robin. 'You do do exciting things, Run-About. Are *you* going in for the balloon-race?'

'Rather!' said Run-About. 'I nearly won it last year. I got a friendly breeze to puff me very hard.'

'Can *we* go and see the race?' said Betty. 'Say yes, Run-About! What time will it be?'

'It's in the afternoon,' said the little brownie.

'We could come!' said Betty. 'Mother's going to see Granny then, and she's not going to take us. We could come!'

'All right. I'll fetch you,' said Run-About. 'But you'll have to look after yourselves, because I shall be up in my balloon. Perhaps you'll bring me luck!'

Chapter 14

Off to the Balloon-Races

Betty and Robin could hardly wait till Friday. They looked out some of the old balloons they had had at their last party and blew them up.

'We'll have a little balloon-race ourselves in the garden!' said Betty. 'You take the two red ones, Robin, I'll have the blue ones. We'll throw them up into the wind and see whose balloons reach the other end of the garden first!'

The wind took the balloons along fast, bouncing and bumping them through the air. Betty's blue one won.

'It won because I had blown it up so big,' she said. 'That's why it won!'

They asked Run-About what colour balloon he was going to race in.

'Yellow,' he said. 'I've got it put away carefully at home. We'll get it on our way to the races.'

When Friday came the children rushed off with Run-About in the little wooden train. They trundled through Fairyland till they came to Run-About's little cottage. There were still no doors to be seen, but Run-About soon altered that!

Just as he had done before, he pencilled a little door in the wall, and hey presto, it was a real door! He knocked and went in.

'Why do you knock?' said Robin.

'Just to see if I'm at home!' said Run-About, and that made the children giggle. He went to a chest and opened the lid. Inside lay a big piece of wrinkled-up yellow rubber – his balloon! He took it out and tucked it under his arm.

'I'm glad I remembered where I put it!' he said. 'Come along – we mustn't be late.'

Out they went, and he slammed the door. It vanished at once. *What* a fine way of making sure that no burglars could get in!

Off they went again in the wooden train

and soon came to the field where the balloon-races were to be held. There were hundreds of little folk there, all very excited.

Run-About went to the starting-point, and shook out his yellow rubber balloon. 'Are you going to blow it up?' asked Robin. 'You will need a lot of breath!'

'Oh – I just pop a Blow-Up spell into the neck of the balloon,' said Run-About. 'Look!'

He popped a tiny blue pellet into the neck of the balloon and blew on it. At once there came a hissing sound and the balloon began to fill with air!

'I wish I had a spell like that when we give a party and I have to blow up all the balloons,' said Robin. 'You really do have such good ideas in Fairyland!'

Run-About turned to watch someone else's balloon being blown up by a spell. His own grew bigger and bigger and bigger – simply enormous! Betty watched it in admiration. How much bigger would it go? Surely it would burst if it grew much bigger?

'Run-About – don't you think you ought to stop your Blow-Up spell now?' she called. 'Run-About swung round to look at his balloon, and he gave a shout.

'My goodness – it'll burst. Stop, Blow-Up spell!'

But he was just too late. The balloon was almost as big as a cottage! It wobbled a little – and then burst with a most tremendous BANG! Everybody fell down flat. The balloon disappeared completely except for a few bits of yellow rubber flying through the air.

Run-About sat up, and tears came into his eyes.

'My beautiful balloon! Why didn't I watch it carefully? Now I can't go in for the race. It was my only balloon.'

'Oh Run-About – I *am* sorry!' said Betty. 'Can't you buy one anywhere?'

Robin suddenly put his hand in his pocket. He had remembered that he had stuffed his and Betty's balloons there, when he had let the air out of them after their little garden race.

'Run-About – have one of mine!' he called, excitedly. 'Look, take this blue one, it blows up nice and big!'

Run-About came over to him in excitement. 'My word – do you mean to say you actually brought your own balloons in your pocket! What a bit of luck. Yes, I'd like that blue one, please – you told me how well it blew away in the wind!'

He pushed a little Blow-Up spell into the balloon's neck, and then blew on it. The children watched it slowly swell up, bigger and bigger and bigger!

'Watch it, watch it!' said Robin. 'Its skin is looking thin now. It may burst!'

But it didn't! Run-About stopped the Blow-Up spell at exactly the right moment.

He ran to get the little baskets that each racing balloonist had to tie underneath with rope. He soon attached his and got into it at the starting-line.

All the racers had to hold tightly to a piece of rope stretched across the field, or their balloons would have gone up into the air at once, the wind was so strong!

'One – two – three – GO!' shouted a voice, and every racer let go the starting-rope.

'Good luck, Run-About, good luck!' shouted the children. 'We do hope you'll fly farther than anyone else. Good luck!'

Run-About's balloon had shot high into the air and the wind took it nicely. Would it win the race? Mind that holly-bush, Run-About! Fly, balloon, fly fast!

Chapter 15

Happy Ending

There came a little rattling noise beside the children, and Robin looked round. It was the wooden engine!

'Oh Betty – the engine wants us to get in so that we can follow the balloons!' said Robin. So in they both got and the little train rattled away over the countryside after the balloons. There were altogether twelve in the race.

Pop! One blew against a pine-tree and the pine needles pricked it! Bang! Another blew against a tall holly-tree and that was the end of that.

A third one began to go down flat, and then two more. 'Only seven left now, and Run-About is second,' said Robin, looking up from the little train.

Bang! Bang! Two more burst. That left five. Then one drifted right down to the ground instead of flying. That left four.

Bang! Oh, dear, was that Run-About's? No, it was another blue balloon that had gone pop. Only three left – and look, one was gradually going down, smaller and smaller. Ah, that was out of the race too.

Now only Run-About's blue balloon was left and a big green one. Run-About was second, but soon a little wind found him and blew him into first place.

The wooden train rattled on, following the two balloons, and behind it came all kinds of coaches and cars carrying little folk who meant to see the finish!

'Oh! Run-About's balloon is beginning to go down – it's getting smaller!' cried Betty, in dismay. She was right – it was already much smaller! Oh, dear!

'The *green* balloon's going down now, too!' shouted someone behind. So it was. What an excitement!

The green balloon kept valiantly up to the blue one, though each was now getting very much smaller, and was drifting down towards the ground. The green one got caught in a bush, and before it could get free Run-About's balloon had gone a good way ahead. But it was going down very fast now, and was a very tiny little thing!

The green balloon sailed on again. The blue one came down to earth, quite flat, and lay there as if it were tired out. Everyone began to shout.

'The green one will win! It's almost up to the blue one. It's winning!'

But no – just a few yards behind Run-About's blue balloon the green one collapsed and dropped down to the grass. It couldn't float even a yard further.

'Run-About's won! The blue balloon has won!' shouted everyone. 'It got further than the green one! Hurrah for Run-About, he's won at last!'

Run-About looked very pleased indeed. He came over to Robin and Betty. 'It was all because of you and your fine balloon!' he said. 'I wouldn't have won in my yellow one, I'm sure. Thank you very much!'

'What's the prize?' asked Robin, as they trundled back to the starting-point in the little wooden train.

'It's a Magic Sweet-Bag,' said Run-About.

'Whatever's that?' asked Betty.

'Just a little paper bag of sweets, which is never empty, however many you eat,' said Run-About.

'What a wonderful prize!' said Robin. 'A sweet-bag that is always full of sweets!'

'Yes – you can wish for any kind you like,' said Run-About. 'Ah – here we are!'

Everyone clapped Run-About as he went to receive the prize. He came straight back

to the children. He held out the sweet-bag, which looked nice and full.

'Here you are!' he said. 'It's for you! You have helped me such a lot while I've stayed in your playroom, and I want you to have this as a little gift from me! You'll love it.'

'Oh, *thank* you, Run-About!' said the children, hardly believing their ears. A magic sweet-bag was never empty – why, there couldn't be a more wonderful present than that!

It certainly was marvellous. The children enjoyed it very much indeed for the next few days. It didn't matter what they wished for – chocolates, toffees, peppermints, fudge – the bag was always full of whatever sweets they wanted!

It was sad to say goodbye to Run-About when his holiday came to an end. He cleaned up the doll's house nicely before he went, and polished the wooden train.

'Please, *please* come and see us whenever you can!' begged Betty. 'We shall miss you dreadfully. When shall we see you again, Run-About?'

'It's my birthday soon, so you must come to my party,' said the little brownie, his green eyes twinkling at them. 'I'll send you an invitation. You'll see me often. If ever I want to borrow any of your toys, I'll come and ask you.'

'Please do!' said Robin. 'And if we want to see you *very* badly, we'll somehow find a way into Fairyland.'

'I'm going now,' said Run-About. 'Goodbye – and thank you for all you've done for me. I've loved it.'

'Take the wooden engine to get back in,' said Robin. Run-About shook his head.

'No. I'll walk down the rabbit-hole, thank you. It's not really very far.'

Off he went, and the two children were sad to see him go. What a wonderful time they had had with him – and what a good thing they had had so many toys they could lend him!

Betty looked as if she was going to cry. But Robin knew how to stop that! He took up the Magic Sweet-Bag and opened it.

'Have a sweet!' he said. 'Cheer up, Betty – we're going to the birthday party – we know the way to Fairyland – and we've got a Magic Sweet-Bag! We're very, very lucky!'

So they are! Don't you think so?